THE BLOSSOMING OF A WALLFLOWER

Laura Shenton

THE BLOSSOMING
OF A WALLFLOWER

Laura Shenton

Iridescent Toad Publishing

Iridescent Toad Publishing.

©Laura Shenton 2024
All rights reserved.

Laura Shenton asserts the moral right to be identified as the author of this work.

No part of this publication may be
reproduced, stored or transmitted in any form or by any means, electronic, mechanical, photocopying, recording, scanning, or otherwise without written permission from the publisher. It is illegal to copy this book, post it to a website, or distribute it by any other means without permission.

This book is entirely a work of fiction. The names, characters and incidents portrayed in it are the work of the author's imagination. Any resemblance to actual persons, living or dead, events or localities is entirely coincidental.

Designations used by companies to distinguish their products are often claimed as trademarks. All brand names and product names used in this book and on its cover are trade names, service marks, trademarks and registered trademarks of their respective owners. The publishers and the book are not associated with any product or vendor mentioned in this book. None of the companies referenced within the book have endorsed the book.

All cover images used under a commercial license.

First edition. ISBN: 978-1-913779-10-8

Chapter One

Sunlight dappled the manicured lawn, casting playful patterns across the ground as Claudia took a delicate sip of her fragrant tea, savouring its warmth and comfort. Seated on sturdy outdoor chairs with plush cushions, beneath the grand, spreading branches of an ancient oak tree, she glanced across the china teacups and polished silverware that adorned the intricately embroidered lace tablecloth. The scene was like something out of a pastoral painting, perfect in its tranquillity. A gentle breeze rustled the leaves overhead, carrying with it the sweet scent of blossoming roses that surrounded the magnificent country manor that she and her family called home.

"Terrance was truly wonderful when I came down with that dreadful cold last week," Emily gushed, her eyes sparkling with happiness as she reached for another dainty cucumber sandwich. "He's so attentive and considerate. He always makes sure I'm happy and well cared for. I feel much better now."

Claudia's older sister by three years, twenty-three-year-old Emily had married Lord Terrance Bathory four years ago. As she brought the sandwich to her mouth, her fingers, adorned with delicate rings, moved with the grace of a woman who had never known hardship.

Emily was dressed in a pale blue muslin gown that accentuated her slender figure, her dark hair neatly arranged in an elegant chignon. Her demeanour radiated confidence and contentment, the epitome of a happily married woman.

Lady Beatrice Florence, their mother, nodded approvingly, her stern features softened by the faintest hint of a smile. Her posture, as always, was impeccable, her presence commanding respect. Clad in a rich maroon silk dress with intricate lace detailing, she exuded an air of authority.

"Indeed, my dear," she told Emily. "You've

made a fine match. We can only hope that Claudia will be as fortunate in securing a suitable husband this season."

Claudia felt a familiar pang of inadequacy as she lowered her gaze to the teacup cradled in her hands. The intricate pattern of roses and gold trim seemed to taunt her, reminding her of the perfection she could never quite achieve. She knew her mother and sister meant well, but their words served as a reminder of the expectations weighing heavily upon her.

"Really, Claudia," Emily continued, her voice light and airy as if discussing the weather, oblivious to her sister's discomfort, "you must put yourself out there more. Be bold and make an effort to engage with people. Who knows what charming young man you might capture the attention of?"

"Your sister is right," Beatrice chimed in firmly, her tone brooking no argument. "The London season will be our best chance to secure your future, and we mustn't squander it."

"And you mustn't be so shy, Claudia," said

Emily. "Put yourself forward, and you'll see how quickly people will take notice."

"You have much to offer, Claudia," Beatrice agreed, "but if you continue to hide your light under a bushel, no one will ever see it."

Claudia, dressed in a lavender gown that matched her soft, introspective nature, forced a polite smile and murmured her agreement. She fought to keep her insecurities at bay. Would she ever be enough? Would anyone ever see her as more than just a plain, uninteresting girl? The teacup in her hand seemed heavier with every passing second, its delicate balance mirroring the precariousness of her emotions.

"Bravo, Mr Bathory!" Emily called out, raising her teacup in a playful salute. "You never cease to amaze with your prowess on the field."

Taking a sip of her tea, Emily gazed admiringly at the distant figure of her husband, who was playing bowls on another part of the lawn; a man of twenty-six, he moved with ease and confidence, every gesture a testament to his refinement and dexterity. His tall, athletic form was dressed in a well-tailored dark green coat and cream breeches, his hair a rich chestnut brown that caught the sunlight.

Claudia watched idly as Terrance carefully assessed the distance to the jack. He then expertly sent a bowl rolling across the smooth grass. With a quiet concentration on his face, his dedication to mastering the game was evident, even in solitary practice. Each roll of the bowl was deliberate, his movements controlled and precise, a display of his natural athleticism and focus. The rhythmic clatter of the bowls and the occasional thud as they gently collided provided a soothing backdrop to the peaceful afternoon.

Despite how talk of the upcoming season stirred a measure of anxiety within her, Claudia couldn't deny the slight flicker of excitement she felt at the thought of attending. It was an opportunity to escape the confines of the country estate, to see and experience the bustling social scene of London. Besides, she knew that refusing to go was not an option. Since the death of her father when she was just a child, her mother and sister had been her primary guides in navigating the expectations of their world. With her father gone, it was imperative for Claudia to find a suitable match, someone who could provide for her and ensure her place in society.

She sighed inwardly, knowing that the season represented a blend of promise and pressure; a chance for happiness, but also a test of her worth. At twenty years old, she was acutely aware of the invisible clock ticking away, each passing day a reminder of her advancing age in the eyes of society. She knew that the prime of a young woman's life was fleeting, and that should she fail to find a suitor, her chances would only diminish. There was an unspoken rule that a woman of her standing must secure a husband by a certain age, lest she be deemed unmarriageable and destined for a life of spinsterhood.

Sipping her tea and listening to her sister and mother discuss her prospects, a deep-seated worry gnawed at Claudia. The thought of facing another season without success filled her with dread. What if she remained a wallflower, overlooked and passed by as the younger debutantes dazzled the eligible bachelors with their fresh beauty and vivacious spirits?

"Here he comes," Emily said happily.

As Terrance approached, his eyes met Emily's with adoration, a silent conversation passing between them that unwittingly served to exacerbate Claudia's feelings of inadequacy.

His presence seemed to light up the space around him, his easy laughter and engaging manner effortlessly drawing attention. He greeted Beatrice, then Claudia, with a pleasant smile, bowing slightly as he took Emily's hand.

"Ladies, I trust you are enjoying this beautiful day?"

"Terrance, dear, you must join us," said Emily, her face lighting up with joy as she responded to her adoring husband. "We were just discussing the upcoming season in London, and how Claudia should make the most of it."

Terrance turned to Claudia, his eyes kind and understanding.

"You have so much to offer, Claudia. I'm sure you will make quite an impression."

Despite his pleasant words, Claudia's heart felt heavy. She managed a weak smile, polite in her acknowledgement of Terrance and his efforts at reassurance. Inside, however, her doubts continued to churn. As the conversation flowed around her, she couldn't shake the feeling of being out of place, like an outsider looking in.

Chapter Two

The setting sun cast a golden glow upon the opulent chamber as Claudia sat by her window. Filigree curtains danced in the evening breeze, their delicate patterns casting intricate shadows on the richly adorned walls. The room was a testament to the Florence family fortune, with ornate furnishings and priceless artwork that spoke of generations of wealth.

"Another day gone," Claudia mused, her fingers idly tracing the fine embroidery on the cushioned window seat beside her.

As she looked at the sprawling gardens below, memories of a time long past flickered through her mind like fragments of a dream.

"I remember when we were children..." she murmured to herself, recalling the laughter and carefree days spent playing amongst the flowers.

But even then, there had been shadows lurking just beneath the surface – moments of cruel mockery that had cut deeper than any blade.

She shuddered as an image of a boy from her childhood surfaced in her memory. She could still feel the slimy, wriggling sensation of a frog sliding down the back of her dress, and how the shock of its touch had caused her to let out a shrill scream. And rather than coming to her aid, Emily had joined in the laughter that echoed around them, her beloved sister's betrayal making the humiliation all the more unbearable.

"Surely things must have changed?" Claudia whispered. "I should hope that I am no longer the awkward, gawky girl that everyone once tormented."

But even as she tried to convince herself, doubt ebbed at the edges of her resolve. The upcoming season in London loomed over her like a gathering storm, threatening to expose her insecurities for all to see.

"What if nothing has changed?" she wondered aloud, her chest tightening with anxiety. "What if I am still the same laughingstock?"

The thought was almost too much to bear, and for a moment, Claudia felt as though she was drowning in a sea of self-doubt.

"Miss Florence?" said a soft female voice.

The gentle tap on Claudia's chamber door broke through the haze of her thoughts, and she turned to see Jemima, her loyal maid, standing hesitantly in the doorway.

The familiar sight of Jemima's kind brown eyes and neatly pinned chestnut hair brought a small measure of relief to Claudia's troubled mind.

"Jemima," she said, her voice wavering slightly. "Please, come in. I would like your company."

"Are you quite all right, Miss Florence?"

Jemima's face was a picture of concern as she stepped into the grand room. The same age as Claudia, in her three years of service to the Florence family, she had become more than just a household attendant – she was a trusted confidante and steadfast friend. She had formed a close bond with Claudia almost from the moment she had entered their home. Despite the differences in their social standing, they had shared many moments together, talking about their hopes and fears, and offering each other solace and encouragement. Jemima's presence was a comforting constant in Claudia's life – a steadying influence that she could always rely on.

"I... I was just thinking about the upcoming season in London," Claudia admitted, her hands wringing together nervously in her lap. "I fear I may be ill-prepared."

"Miss Florence, you are more than capable of handling whatever comes your way," Jemima reassured. "Remember, you have faced greater challenges before, and you have always emerged stronger for it."

"Have I? Or has my past merely been a series of humiliations, each more painful than the last?"

Claudia's eyes shimmered with unshed tears, her vulnerability laid bare before her dear maid.

"Miss Florence, you mustn't think like that," Jemima urged gently.

"Jemima, I must ask you something, and I need you to be perfectly honest with me," Claudia began, a note of insecurity in her tone. "With the season in London approaching, I cannot help but worry... am I ugly?"

"Miss Florence!" Jemima exclaimed, shocked by the question. "You are far from..."

"Jemima, please," Claudia interrupted, her eyes imploring. "You are my friend, not just my maid. I want the truth, not what you think I want to hear."

Jemima searched Claudia's face for a moment, and then nodded with certainty.

"Very well, Miss Florence. The truth is, I have always thought you to be beautiful and worthy. You possess a grace that many women can only dream of."

"But if what you say is true, and if I am not as plain as I have always believed, then why... why have I never felt beautiful?"

Jemima paused for a moment, her expression thoughtful as she considered Claudia's question. Finally, she spoke with a gentle wisdom that belied her years.

"Miss Florence, I believe that it is difficult for any person to truly see the beauty in themselves. We are often our own harshest critic, focusing on every perceived flaw instead of the many lovely qualities we possess. Perhaps the assurance you seek is something that will come with time, as you learn to accept and love yourself as others do."

Although touched by Jemima's good intentions, Claudia remained unconvinced. Highly aware of this, the kind maid breathed out a heavy sigh.

"Miss Florence," Jemima ventured after a while, her voice lighter, "I want you to know that I will do everything within my power to support you during the London season. You deserve to feel comfortable and confident, and I shall be by your side every step of the way. I shall ensure that you are impeccably attired and at ease for any event of the season. Together, we will navigate the whirlwind of London society. I have no doubt that you will shine."

Jemima's words inspired a sense of possibility, momentarily banishing the shadows of self-doubt that had taken up residence in Claudia's mind; as she gazed at her loyal maid, she marvelled at the depth of their bond.

"Thank you, Jemima," Claudia said earnestly, her voice barely able to convey the magnitude of her appreciation. "Your support means more to me than I can express. I find it far easier to confide in you than in Mother or Emily. I am ever so grateful for your unwavering friendship."

"It is my honour and pleasure to be there for you, Miss Florence," Jemima said with genuine affection. "You are far more deserving of happiness than you give yourself credit for."

Chapter Three

Beneath a sky of dove grey and gossamer clouds, the carriage trundled along the winding country road, its polished wood exterior gleaming in the muted sunlight. The passing countryside presented an idyllic picture of rural England, belying the inner storm of Claudia's anxiety.

Inside the carriage, Claudia sat across from her mother, the plush velvet upholstery cushioning them as the wheels rattled over uneven ground. The scent of lavender sachets mingled with the faint aroma of horseflesh and damp earth, carried through the open window by a breeze that rustled the tassels of the silk curtains.

"London awaits us, my dear," Beatrice said, her voice crisp and authoritative as she smoothed her skirt with gloved hands, "and with it, the opportunity to secure you a suitable match."

Claudia swallowed the unease that bubbled up within her, her gaze fixed on the rolling green hills that seemed to stretch endlessly around them. She could feel her mother's stern eyes upon her, studying her as though she were an unpolished gemstone awaiting refinement.

"Yes, Mother," Claudia answered quietly, her fingers fidgeting with the lace trim of her sleeves.

"Remember," Beatrice continued, her tone admonishing, "Emily has set an excellent example for you to follow. You must be approachable, endearing, and above all, attentive to the needs of those around you. A lady who captures the hearts of others will have no shortage of suitors vying for her hand in marriage."

Claudia nodded, trying her best to quell the mounting anxiety that threatened to overwhelm her. She knew all too well the weight of expectations that rested upon her shoulders, the legacy of success that she was expected to uphold. Deep down, she couldn't help but doubt her ability to meet such lofty standards. What if she failed? What if she proved herself unworthy of the love and admiration that seemed to come so easily to Emily?

"Are you listening, Claudia?" Beatrice asked, her voice cutting sharply through her daughter's reverie.

"Of course, Mother," Claudia replied, forcing a smile onto her lips as she met her mother's gaze. "I shall endeavour to make you proud."

"See that you do," said Beatrice, her expression softening ever so slightly as she reached out to pat Claudia's hand. "You are a Florence, after all – we Florences always rise to the occasion."

As the conversation dragged on, Claudia tried her best to remain engaged. Despite this, her thoughts continued to spiral into the dark corners of self-doubt. What if she failed to attract a suitor? What if her insecurities held her back from finding love? The idea of ending up alone, forever relegated to the role of spinster, was more upsetting than she dared to admit.

"Dearest Mother," Claudia hesitantly pondered, her voice barely above a whisper. "Do you truly believe there is someone out there for me?"

Her expression inscrutable, Beatrice studied her daughter for a moment.

"Of course, my dear," she replied, her tone softened by the slightest hint of compassion. "But you must be willing to put in the effort – to present yourself in the best possible light."

Doing her best to dignify her mother's optimism with a response, Claudia nodded, swallowing the lump in her throat. As the carriage continued its journey through the beautiful English countryside, she stared out of the window, her thoughts consumed by the daunting task that lay ahead.

As the hours passed, the countryside's gentle charm was replaced by the more structured landscape of the city's outskirts. The open fields gave way to clusters of cottages with smoke curling from their chimneys, and children playing by the dusty roadside. Claudia took in the changing scenery with a sense of bittersweet nostalgia. She loved the peace and beauty of the countryside, whilst the prospect of the London season filled her with anticipation.

The air grew heavier with the scent of industry and the distant hum of urban life. Trees lined the road less frequently, and the expanse of green was broken by cobblestone streets and rows of tightly packed townhouses. The sky seemed to shrink, hemmed in by rooftops and chimneys, as the carriage rolled ever closer into the city.

As they crossed the Thames and entered the bustling streets of London proper, the transformation was complete. The tranquil sounds of nature were no more, and had been replaced by the cacophony of city life. Vendors shouted their wares, carriages clattered over the roads, and people bustled about with determined energy. Tall buildings loomed on either side, casting long shadows that danced in the late afternoon light.

It had been a year since Claudia had last set foot in London. As she peered out of the window, the city's vibrancy was both overwhelming and exhilarating. Everything seemed alive with movement, a stark contrast to the serene landscapes of home.

As the carriage wound its way through the crowded streets, past large townhouses and shops, Claudia couldn't help but feel a flicker of hope. The city held possibilities that the countryside could not, and perhaps, just perhaps, this season would bring her the happiness she so desperately sought.

When the carriage came to a halt with a gentle jostle, it roused Claudia from her brooding reverie. Her breath caught in her throat at the sight that greeted her: a grand city house that seemed to embody every ounce of opulence. Its façade boasted tall windows framed by ornate stonework.

"Here we are, my dear," Beatrice announced with satisfaction, her eyes sweeping over their temporary residence. "The London season awaits."

Chapter Four

The footman swiftly stepped forward, opening the carriage door with practiced precision. Beatrice, ever poised, accepted his assistance with a regal nod, her gloved hand resting lightly on his for balance as she descended. Claudia followed, her own steps more tentative but no less graceful.

The building before them was a marvel of architecture. Ivy climbed artfully up the walls, and the entrance was framed by imposing columns. The early evening light cast a glow on the pale stone, enhancing its grandeur and making the scene almost ethereal.

Claudia paused at the foot of the steps, taking in the sight of their temporary home. It had been a year since she had last seen it.

It seemed even more magnificent than she remembered. Flower boxes overflowing with vibrant blooms added a touch of colour to the stately exterior, softening its formidable presence. The building loomed large, not just in size, but in significance. It represented opportunity and pressure, hope and expectation. The grandeur of the residence was a stark reminder of the world that Claudia was about to re-enter – a world of social manoeuvring and potential alliances, where every action could shape her future.

"Welcome back to London, Claudia," said Beatrice, turning around to address her daughter, a kindness in her tone. "This season will be crucial for you."

Claudia nodded in agreement, and then, after taking a deep breath, ascended the steps beside her mother, feeling the weight of her skirts swishing around her ankles. The footman swung open the grand doors, revealing a lavish foyer bathed in the soft glow of crystal chandeliers. Claudia couldn't help but feel a shiver of both excitement and apprehension. This house, so magnificent and awe-inspiring, would be their home for the coming months – a backdrop to the pivotal events of the season.

Claudia's heart skipped a beat as she and her mother crossed the threshold into the grand house. The entrance hall was a vision of opulence, with gilded mirrors and intricate frescoes adorning the walls, reflecting the flickering light of the crystal chandelier above. Jemima, who had arrived earlier to prepare the house, greeted them with a smile that brought some comfort to Claudia amidst the overwhelming grandeur.

"Welcome, Lady Florence, Miss Florence," Jemima said, curtseying humbly. "I trust your journey was pleasant? I have taken great care to ensure that everything is ready for you."

"Thank you, Jemima," Beatrice replied, her gaze sweeping over the impeccably polished marble floors and elaborate furnishings. "I expect nothing less. Now, please show us around. We must reacquaint ourselves with our surroundings."

"Of course, ma'am," Jemima said.

As Jemima led them through the maze of opulent chambers, Claudia couldn't help but marvel at the sheer size and extravagance of the place. Each room seemed more exquisite than the last, with ornate ceilings, plush velvet drapes, and fine tapestries that spoke of generations of wealth and refinement. In the drawing room, delicate porcelain figurines lined the shelves, while an exquisite grand piano stood proudly by the floor-to-ceiling windows. The dining hall was equally impressive, boasting a mahogany table capable of seating twenty guests in its gleaming splendour.

"Here we have the library, Miss Florence," Jemima announced.

The maid opened a set of double doors to reveal a haven of leather-bound books and cosy armchairs. A fire crackled merrily in the hearth, casting a pleasant glow over the room.

"It's magnificent," said Beatrice, a note of pride in her voice. "Just think of the dinner parties and soirées we shall host here. Our name will be on everyone's lips."

"Indeed, Mother," Claudia replied softly, her attention lingering on the inviting shelves of books that would surely provide solace from the relentless whirlwind of the season.

"Lastly, let me show you to your chamber, Miss Florence," Jemima said.

The maid guided the two women up a grand staircase adorned with plush red carpets and exquisite paintings. As they reached the top, she opened a door to reveal a spacious room bathed in the softness of the early evening light. A canopied bed, dressed in luxurious linens, took centre stage. A large vanity, complete with a gilded mirror and an array of brushes and perfumes, hinted at the social commitments that would await Claudia in the coming weeks.

"Thank you, Jemima," Claudia murmured, a little daunted, but impressed.

Taking in every detail of the room that would be her sanctuary throughout the season, Claudia couldn't deny the beauty of her surroundings. Yet, as her mother's expectations weighed heavily upon her, she couldn't help but feel fragile amidst the grandeur.

"Take some time to rest, Claudia," Beatrice advised, noting the slight furrow in her daughter's brow. "The season awaits, and we must be prepared for all it has to offer."

"Of course, Mother," Claudia acquiesced, offering a small, weary smile.

"Good. Now, I shall retire to my own chamber, but remember: we are not here merely to pass the time. This is our chance to secure your future, and we must seize it with both hands."

With that, Beatrice swept from the room, leaving Claudia to contemplate the challenges that lay ahead in the glittering world beyond her sumptuous sanctuary.

Chapter Five

The grand dining hall of the Florence's London residence shimmered in a golden haze as candles flickered on the elaborately set table with its pristine white cloth and gleaming silverware. An impressive crystal chandelier hung above, casting an ethereal glow on the guests below. Rich burgundy draperies framed the tall windows, giving way to a breathtaking view of the moonlight. The scent of roasted pheasant and exotic spices mingled with the delicate bouquet of roses that adorned the table.

Sitting quietly at the table, Claudia was transfixed on her mother, who was holding court with their esteemed guests. Her voice was firm and modulated, her words carefully chosen to keep the conversation flowing seamlessly. It seemed as though even the most obstinate of guests could not resist the charisma of Lady Beatrice Florence.

"Ah, Lord Cunningham," she graciously addressed one of the gentlemen, "I trust you are enjoying your time in London? I've heard the theatre season is particularly splendid this year."

"Indeed, it is, Lady Florence," he replied with enthusiasm. "I had the pleasure of attending a performance just last week that was most captivating."

"Is that so?" Beatrice said, her interest piqued as she continued to expertly engage him in conversation about the plays and performers he had enjoyed.

Claudia marvelled at her mother's ability to captivate those around her, but her heart sank with the realisation that she lacked the same self-assurance. Allowing her gaze to wander across the room, Claudia took in the numerous handsome faces that filled the grand space. Each one seemed more dashing and eligible than the next, yet the thought of initiating a conversation with any of them left her feeling weak and vulnerable. The fear of rejection and the possibility of becoming the subject of ridicule plagued her mind, keeping her firmly rooted in her seat.

"Would you care for more wine, Miss Florence?" a footman asked, breaking her reverie.

"Thank you, yes," Claudia replied politely, offering him her glass.

As the evening wore on, she found herself becoming increasingly withdrawn, the lively chatter around her only serving to highlight her insecurities. The dining hall was abundant with the sounds of laughter and animated conversation. It flowed around her, filled with the latest gossip, plans for the season, and lighthearted banter. As silverware clinked against fine china, she could hardly focus on the culinary delights before her.

She glanced at Emily and Terrance, seated across the table, their love for one another evident in the tender exchanges that passed between them – a gentle touch here, a whispered endearment there. Emily's eyes sparkled with happiness as she leaned in to speak softly to her husband, her smile radiant and genuine. Terrance's focus never strayed far from his wife, his admiration clear in every glance.

Claudia ached with a deep, unspoken longing. It was a bond she yearned to experience for herself, yet the thought of seeking it out seemed insurmountable. Her focus drifted to her plate, the carefully arranged food barely touched. She felt like an outsider, her presence almost an intrusion in this world of effortless grandeur and easy confidence. Would she ever be able to navigate these social waters? The season ahead would be full of endless rounds of balls, soirées, and social calls. It all felt like a mountain that she was ill-prepared to climb.

"Please excuse me," Claudia murmured to nobody in particular, rising from her seat as discreetly as possible. "I find myself in need of some fresh air."

Under the watchful gaze of her mother, who declined to leave the conversation she had already committed to, Claudia made her way out onto the balcony. Once there, she took deep breaths of the cool night air to steady her nerves. The scent of blooming roses wafted towards her, filling her senses with their sweet fragrance. As she looked at the stars above, she wondered if any of the eligible men of the season would be capable of seeing her for the woman she truly was.

She leaned against the stone balustrade, the polished surface cold beneath her fingers. The garden below was bathed in the soft glow of the moonlight, casting elongated shadows that danced with the gentle sway of the trees. For a moment, she allowed herself to escape the pressures and expectations that weighed so heavily upon her. As she stood there, the distant murmur of the dinner party fading into the background, her thoughts began to drift to memories of her father.

He had passed away when she was just a young girl, but his presence in her life had been profound and loving. She could still recall the sound of his laughter, a pleasant, rich timbre that could fill a room and make her feel safe and cherished. He had been a man of kindness and strength, his demeanour always calm and reassuring.

Claudia remembered the afternoons they had spent together in the gardens of their country estate. He would tell her stories of knights and adventures, his voice weaving tales that sparked her imagination and made her feel invincible. She could still picture his face, the way his eyes crinkled at the corners when he smiled, and the gentle way he would tuck a stray lock of hair behind her ear.

The loss of her father had left a void in her heart, one that no amount of time or comfort could ever truly heal. She missed his guidance, his wisdom, and the unconditional love he had bestowed upon her. As she stood alone beneath the vast night sky, the ache of his absence felt particularly sharp.

Claudia's mother had done her best to fill the role of both parents, but the weight of responsibility and societal expectation often overshadowed the tenderness Claudia had once known. Beatrice's love was real, but was expressed in the strictures of propriety and ambition, leaving Claudia to navigate the complexities of her emotions on her own.

Claudia sighed, her breath visible in the cool air. She wondered what advice her father might give her now if he were here. Would he see potential in her? Would he encourage her to be bold, to seek out the love and happiness she so deeply craved? Or would he simply hold her, reassuring her that she was enough no matter what?

The stars above twinkled faintly, distant and unobtainable, much like how Claudia's dreams seemed at times. She felt tears she hadn't realised were there, and quickly wiped them away with a trembling hand. She longed for the comfort of her father's embrace, the sense of security that his presence had always brought.

She knew she couldn't linger on the balcony much longer. The chill of the night air was creeping into her bones, but more than that, she understood the importance of her presence at the dinner table. To remain outside would risk offending her mother or causing unnecessary worry. Beatrice, with her keen sense of propriety and expectation, would not take kindly to an extended absence.

Claudia took a deep breath, the crisp air filling her lungs and steadying her resolve. She straightened her shoulders, and smoothed the fabric of her dress with deliberate care. Steeling herself, she stoically did her best to push her fears and insecurities to the back of her mind. Then, with measured steps, she turned around to head back inside.

Chapter Six

A few days after the dinner party, in the twilight hours of a fine summer's evening, Claudia stood in her chamber of the Florence's London residence, preparing for the first ball of the season. The sky outside her window was awash with hues of pink and orange, the colours blending softly as the sun dipped below the horizon. The room was bathed in the gentle glow of a crystal chandelier, its light refracting through the prisms and casting a shimmering radiance across the walls.

Jemima bustled around the room, her movements purposeful and efficient. Tonight, her role was to transform Claudia into a vision of elegance that would befit the grandeur of the upcoming occasion.

"Let's start with the corset," she said, her voice soothing.

Her nerves tingling, Claudia stepped towards the intricately designed garment that Jemima was holding up. The corset was a masterpiece of fine lace and delicate boning, its craftsmanship evident in every stitch. As Claudia positioned herself, Jemima moved behind her, her fingers skilled and precise. With practiced ease, Jemima began tightening the laces, drawing them steadily through the eyelets.

The corset cinched Claudia's waist, inch by inch, creating the desired silhouette that fashion dictated. With each pull, Claudia felt the garment's firm embrace, its constriction both shaping her figure and limiting her breath.

"Almost there, Miss Florence," Jemima murmured reassuringly as she worked.

Claudia took shallow breaths, trying to steady herself against the discomfort. The final tug secured the corset in place, its structure supporting her posture, but also imposing a rigidity that mirrored the social confines of her world.

"There," Jemima said, tying off the laces with a flourish. "You look lovely already."

Claudia appreciated Jemima's complement, recognising the maid's efforts to bolster her confidence for the night ahead. She knew Jemima was not just performing her duties, but was also trying to inspire a sense of calm. Jemima's unwavering support had become an invaluable source of strength to Claudia, especially in moments like this.

"Thank you, Jemima," Claudia said sincerely. "I don't know what I'd do without you."

"It's my pleasure to help you, Miss Florence. You're going to be wonderful tonight. Just remember to hold your head high."

Moving on to the next task, Jemima helped Claudia into a soft chemise, and then a splendid ball gown, a creation of silk and satin in a rich, emerald green that complemented Claudia's fair complexion. The gown was adorned with delicate lace and tiny pearls, its full skirts cascading to the floor.

"You look stunning, Miss Florence," Jemima said as she smoothed the fabric, ensuring to make every pleat and fold look perfect. "Just wait until everyone sees you."

As she caught sight of herself in the mirror, Claudia barely recognised the reflection of the woman looking back at her. Despite her nerves about the ball, a small spark of excitement flickered within her. The sense of occasion was palpable.

Next, Jemima turned her attention to Claudia's hair. She carefully brushed out the long, dark locks, her touch gentle and reassuring. With practiced skill, she twisted and pinned the hair into an elaborate updo, leaving a few soft curls to frame Claudia's face. The style was fetching yet understated, highlighting Claudia's delicate features.

"There," Jemima said, stepping back to admire her handiwork. "You look wonderful."

Claudia stared at herself in the mirror, the transformation almost complete.

"Thank you, Jemima."

"We're not quite finished," Jemima replied playfully.

The maid reached for the small table of cosmetics. She applied a light touch of powder to Claudia's face, a hint of rouge to her cheeks, and a subtle colour to her lips. The effect was natural yet radiant, enhancing Claudia's beauty without overwhelming it.

Jemima stepped back, surveying her work with satisfaction and pride. She then moved to a small, ornately carved wooden box resting on the vanity. With a delicate touch, she opened it to reveal a pair of pristine white silk gloves, their fabric shimmering softly in the chandelier's light.

"Here you go," she said, her voice gentle as she lifted the gloves from the box, holding them up for Claudia to see. "They will complete your ensemble perfectly."

Claudia's eyes widened slightly as she took in the sight of the gloves. They were exquisite, the silk smooth and luxurious. Jemima smiled as she guided Claudia's hands into them, ensuring that each finger was perfectly placed.

"Remember, Miss Florence," Jemima said confidently as she moved to begin fastening a pair of delicate earrings to Claudia's ears. "You are beautiful just as you are. This ball is just an opportunity for others to see in you what I see every day. Just be yourself, and everything will fall into place."

"I hope you're right," Claudia murmured, her eyes dropping to the delicate lace at her neckline. "I want to believe I can impress tonight, but what if… what if I can't live up to everyone's expectations?"

Jemima paused what she was doing, her expression earnest as she reached out to clasp Claudia's hands in hers.

"Miss Florence, you are more than ready for this. You have a beautiful spirit. Anyone who can't see that, isn't worth your time."

Claudia felt a lump forming in her throat. Jemima's kindness, her unwavering support and genuine encouragement, touched her deeply. The maid had gone above and beyond; not just in her duties, but in her efforts to make Claudia feel not only worthy, but special.

However, as much as she wished to, Claudia simply could not rid herself of the pang of doubt that gnawed at her. She was impressed by how beautifully Jemima had dressed her, yet she couldn't shake the fear that no amount of finery could hide her insecurities. The grandeur of her appearance felt almost like a mask, a fragile façade that could crumble under the scrutiny of the evening.

"Take some deep breaths, Miss Florence," Jemima gently reminded as she fastened a delicate lace fan around Claudia's wrist. "Believe in yourself, and the rest will follow."

Straightening her posture, Claudia took a deep breath, letting the fabric of her gown brush against her skin, a tangible reminder of the effort and care Jemima had put into preparing her for this night. She looked at her reflection once more, seeing not just the outward transformation, but also the kindness and dedication behind it. Jemima's work was a labour of love.

Claudia decided in that moment that, regardless of her lingering insecurities, she owed it to Jemima to try her best to enjoy the ball. The evening was not just a chance to impress, but an opportunity to honour the beautiful job Jemima had done. If nothing else, Claudia would embrace the night for the sake of her loyal maid's tireless efforts.

50

Chapter Seven

Claudia arrived at the grand ballroom, her heart pounding with a blend of anticipation and anxiety. The room was a dazzling spectacle, bathed in the soft glow of countless chandeliers that hung from the high ornate ceiling. Gilded mirrors lined the walls, reflecting the light and creating an illusion of infinite space. Rich, crimson draperies framed tall windows, and the wooden floor was a polished expanse, gleaming underfoot. Musicians in a corner played a lively waltz, their instruments blending harmoniously to fill the air with a melody that seemed to set the entire room in motion.

Taking a cautious step forward into the space, Claudia felt the familiar weight of her mother's gaze upon her almost immediately. Beatrice stood near the entrance, her posture regal and imposing in a gown of deep burgundy silk. Her eyes, sharp and expectant, tracked Claudia's every movement. Claudia knew those eyes well – they spoke volumes without uttering a single word, conveying a silent command to mingle and to be the daughter that Beatrice envisioned, with the same effortless grace that Emily embodied.

Claudia hesitated, her feet feeling as though they were rooted to the spot. Her eyes drifted across the ballroom, finally landing on Emily and her husband. They stood at the far side of the room, engaged in animated conversation with a small group of guests. Terrance, ever the attentive husband, had his arm lightly resting on Emily's waist, his face a picture of adoration as he listened to her speak. Emily, with her natural poise and radiance, appeared completely at ease, her confidence drawing people in like moths to a flame.

Claudia watched them for a moment, a pang of longing tightening her chest. She wasn't sure if Emily had noticed her arrival, but even if she had, Claudia doubted her sister would be interested in engaging with her. Emily had always been somewhat aloof towards

Claudia, their relationship marked by a polite but distant cordiality rather than genuine closeness.

Drawing a deep breath, Claudia looked around at the scene before her. Couples moved buoyantly in time with the music. She felt a wave of unease wash over her, the lively atmosphere only serving to heighten her sense of being out of her depth.

"Claudia, dear," Beatrice said, appearing suddenly beside her daughter, her tone warm but with an underlying firmness. "You look lovely tonight. Remember to hold your head high. Confidence is most imperative."

"Thank you, Mother," Claudia replied, grateful that she was no longer standing alone in a room full of people. "I will try my best."

"That's all I ask, darling," said Beatrice, her tone softening slightly, but her expectations still abundantly clear. "You have everything it takes to make a good impression. Just remember to be engaging. People appreciate a good conversationalist."

Claudia nodded nervously. She knew her mother meant well, but the pressure felt overwhelming.

"I'll do my best," she repeated, trying to summon a confident smile.

Her attention drawn to a group of esteemed guests across the room, Beatrice excused herself from Claudia. As she swept away, her presence commanded attention while she moved to mingle effortlessly with the other attendees.

As Claudia watched her mother, a blend of relief and trepidation washed over her. She felt a sudden wave of vulnerability, standing alone amidst the throng of guests, the soft strains of music providing a backdrop to her solitude.

Drawing a deep breath, she looked around at the swirling figures on the dance floor, their movements synchronised and assured. Her hands, encased in the white silk gloves that Jemima had so carefully presented to her, trembled slightly. She grimaced awkwardly, trying to calm the nervous flutter in her stomach.

Steeling herself, she took another tentative step, further into the room, determined to find a way to enjoy the ball, if only to show herself and those who believed in her that she could rise to the occasion. As the music swelled around her, she hoped that somehow, she could find her place within the rhythm and splendour of the evening.

Just as she was preparing herself to navigate a little further into the ballroom, she suddenly seized with a jolt of anxiety. Across the room, standing under the brilliant glow of a chandelier, was Miss Jacqueline Harcourt. Claudia's pulse quickened at the sight. Miss Harcourt, with her striking auburn hair meticulously styled and her emerald gown accentuating her slender figure, exuded an aura of superiority that could intimidate even the most confident debutante.

Miss Harcourt was the epitome of a socialite, her every movement calculated to draw admiration. Her eyes, a piercing shade of green, scanned the room with a predatory glare, her lips curling into a smile that held no kindness. Claudia knew that look well – it was the same one she had encountered last season, the look that promised unpleasant words and veiled insults.

Her memories of the previous year came flooding back – the whispered comments, the cold, cutting remarks that had left her feeling small and humiliated. She had done nothing to warrant such treatment from Miss Harcourt, but it seemed that the woman took pleasure in finding targets for her cruelty. At twenty, the same age as Claudia, Miss Harcourt wielded her social power with the precision of a sharpened dagger, and Claudia had been one of her victims.

For a moment, Claudia considered retreating for the evening, but she couldn't do that; whatever would her mother say?! She couldn't let fear dictate her actions.

Determined to hold her ground, she lifted her chin slightly, drawing herself up to her full height. However, her efforts were quickly rendered futile when Miss Harcourt and her entourage began to move towards her across the large ballroom. The sight of the small, glittering group felt like an advancing storm, poised to unleash a torrent of disdain. Miss Harcourt led the way, her regal bearing and gregarious stride a stark contrast to Claudia's growing apprehension. The ladies surrounding Miss Harcourt, all dressed in the latest fashions, exchanged amused glances, their laughter tinkling like shards of glass.

Claudia could feel her palms getting clammy beneath her silk gloves. She became acutely aware of every imperfection in her posture, every hesitation in her expression. The memory of last season's cruel remarks echoed in her mind, fuelling her discomfort.

As the group drew closer, Claudia's courage wavered. She could hear snippets of their conversation, laced with the kind of laughter that suggested they were already preparing to dissect her appearance and mannerisms. Claudia's throat tightened. She felt helpless and frozen to the spot. It was as if the very air around her had grown colder, sharper, ready to cut through her.

Desperately, she searched the room for a friendly face, someone to anchor her in this sea of hostility. Unfortunately, Emily and Terrance were too far away, engrossed in their own world, and her mother was nowhere to be seen.

Miss Harcourt's eyes, gleaming with cruel amusement, met Claudia's. Her lips then curved into a smirk that caused Claudia to shudder. It was the same expression that had preceded many a cutting remark.

"What a shame it must be for you, to be stood here all on your own," Miss Harcourt said with feigned concern. "One can only imagine the extent of your trials."

Claudia felt her cheeks burn as she struggled to find a suitable response. Before she could speak, Miss Harcourt continued.

"Perhaps we should introduce you to some gentlemen. I'm sure there must be someone here who would be willing to endure a dance with you."

As the small entourage surrounding Miss Harcourt tittered behind their fans, Claudia fought back tears of humiliation, desperately wishing that she could disappear into the shadows.

It was then that she saw him: a tall, handsome man whose piercing blue eyes seemed to hold a world of stories within them. He strode confidently across the room, his gaze never wavering from the young women surrounding Claudia.

"Good evening, ladies," he said, his voice smooth as silk and tinged with subtle wit. "I couldn't help but overhear your conversation, and I must say, I find your words towards this fair lady to be most unbecoming."

Claudia stood in awe as the women's laughter died in their throats to be replaced by a shocked silence. They stared indignantly at the charismatic stranger.

"Miss, may I have the honour of this dance?" the gentleman asked, extending his hand to Claudia with a caring smile.

"Uh, y-yes," Claudia stammered shyly, placing her trembling hand in his.

As the enigmatic gentleman led her onto the dance floor, Claudia couldn't resist the urge to glance back briefly. Her heart sank when she saw Miss Harcourt standing at the edge of the room, her eyes locked onto her in a glare that could pierce steel. The daggers in Miss Harcourt's stare were unmistakable, a silent promise of disdain and retribution.

Claudia quickly turned around, trying to focus on the dance and the handsome man now leading her.

As they glided across the floor, he endearingly inclined his head slightly.

"May I have the pleasure of knowing the name of my enchanting partner?" he enquired, his voice smooth and refined.

Claudia blushed, her eyes shyly meeting his.

"I am Miss Claudia Florence," she replied, her voice soft yet clear.

"I am delighted to make your acquaintance, Miss Florence," he responded, his grip gentle yet firm as he guided her through the steps of the waltz. "I am Mr Luke Merrifield."

"The pleasure is mine, Mr Merrifield," Claudia said, attempting to steady her nerves. "I must confess, it has been quite some time since I last attended such a grand ball."

Mr Merrifield's eyes twinkled with a hint of amusement.

"You could have fooled me, Miss Florence. You carry yourself so well. One would assume you are quite accustomed to such occasions."

"You are too kind, Mr Merrifield," Claudia replied, feeling both flattered and a little nervous from his compliment. "I fear I am still finding my way amidst all this splendour."

"Then allow me to assist you," Mr Merrifield replied. "I shall consider it my duty to ensure that you enjoy this evening to the fullest."

Claudia's smile widened, a flicker of confidence igniting within her.

"You are most generous, sir," she said gratefully. "I look forward to it."

Chapter Eight

Claudia stood alone at the edge of the grand ballroom, her emotions a blend of anticipation and nerves. The scene was dazzling: crystal chandeliers bathed the room in a golden light, and the soft strains of a string quartet filled the air, mingling with the hum of polite conversation. The ladies, adorned in exquisite gowns, and the gentlemen, resplendent in their evening attire, moved exuberantly about the room, creating a flurry of colour.

Her gloved fingers tightening around the delicate fan in her hand, Claudia scanned the crowd, hoping to spot Mr Luke Merrifield. Ever since she had danced with him at the ball last night, his image had been lingering in her mind – the way he had looked at her, the warmth of his touch as they had moved across the dance floor together. Tonight, she keenly hoped to see him again, to recapture that fleeting connection.

Despite her enthusiasm, however, she firmly told herself that she mustn't get her hopes up too high. It was entirely possible that Mr Merrifield would not attend tonight's ball, and even if he did, there was no guarantee that he would be keen to see her again. She couldn't afford to let herself be consumed by longing for something that might never come to pass.

After all, she reminded herself, he had left the ball in a hurry the previous night, offering only a brief, apologetic smile before disappearing into the throng of guests. The memory of his sudden departure made her feel uncertain. Had something urgent demanded his attention, or had he simply lost interest in her? The latter possibility made her stomach churn with doubt.

Suddenly, a familiar voice broke through her reverie.

"Good evening, Miss Florence."

Claudia turned, startled to find Mr Merrifield

standing at her side, his kind blue eyes gleaming with compassion. For a moment, she was too surprised to speak. She felt a rush of relief and pleasure, so intense that she had to steel herself not to seem overly eager. As her cheeks warmed, she hoped the dim lighting would hide her blush.

"Mr Merrifield," she managed, her voice steady despite the flutter of excitement in her chest. "Good evening."

"Please forgive me for my abrupt departure at our last encounter," he said sincerely, imploring her to understand. "I assure you, it was not my intention to leave you so suddenly."

"Indeed?" Claudia murmured, searching his face for any hint of dishonesty.

"Indeed," he repeated firmly. "Had the situation been less urgent, I would not have dreamt of leaving your side."

Mr Merrifield's steadfastness had caught Claudia off guard, and for a moment, she allowed herself to consider the possibility that he was telling the truth.

"Very well, Mr Merrifield," she said cautiously, still wary, but willing to entertain his explanation. "I shall take you at your word. But you must understand, I have often been the target of ridicule and jest. It is difficult for me to trust that someone like you could truly be interested in a woman like me."

"Miss Florence," Mr Merrifield responded gently, taking her hand, "I can only imagine how painful such experiences must have been for you. However, I assure you, my interest in you is sincere. Your beauty, intelligence, and kindness have captured my attention, and I would be honoured to continue getting to know you better. Come with me outside the ballroom. I promise there is a reasonable explanation for my abrupt departure last night."

Claudia hesitated, torn between her desire for this gentleman and the fear that she might be setting herself up for humiliation. As she met Mr Merrifield's gaze though, there was an earnestness in his eyes that made her want to put her faith in him. Swallowing her trepidation, she allowed him to lead her away from the ballroom.

"Thank you, Miss Florence," Mr Merrifield said as they left the crowded room, his touch steady against her trembling fingers. "I understand your reservations, but I promise you, you have nothing to fear from me."

The grand house seemed to come alive as Mr Merrifield led Claudia through its hallowed halls, each step echoing softly against the marble floors. Crystal chandeliers glittered above them, casting a glow upon the vibrant tapestries that adorned the walls. As they passed an ornate mirror, Claudia caught sight of their reflection – a striking pair, cloaked in mystery and anticipation.

"Have you ever ventured through a grand house like this, Miss Florence?" Mr Merrifield asked, a playful lilt to his voice.

"Only in my dreams," she replied, her gaze wandering over the intricate woodwork and delicate frescoes that seemed to whisper tales of bygone days. "It is truly magnificent."

"Indeed it is," he agreed, guiding her past an imposing grandfather clock that chimed melodiously behind them as they carried on. "Still though, there is something even more astonishing just beyond these walls."

As they reached the threshold of a set of French doors, Claudia's pulse quickened, her curiosity piquing at the promise of what lay beyond. With a gentle touch, Mr Merrifield opened the doors and ushered her outside, the air fragrant with the scent of blossoming flowers.

The moon, along with countless lanterns, cast a glow over the sprawling gardens, bathing them in a light that seemed to soften the edges of reality. Claudia felt as though she had stepped into a world of enchantment, the cold night air a sharp contrast to the stifling humidity inside the ballroom. She shivered slightly, but found herself relishing the sensation.

"Isn't it splendid?" said Mr Merrifield, gesturing towards the sight before them. "A haven from the chaos within."

"It is absolutely breathtaking," Claudia uttered, awestruck by the enchanting scene.

"Miss Florence, I must confess," Mr Merrifield began, "the reason I was so eager to bring you out here was not solely to alleviate your discomfort. It is also because I want to share this moment with you. There is something about the stillness of the night, the beauty of nature, that makes me feel truly alive. I hope that perhaps you might feel the same."

"You are quite perceptive, Mr Merrifield," Claudia admitted, touched by his understanding.

"Allow me to introduce you to my two most trusted companions," he said.

He led Claudia towards a beautifully crafted carriage waiting at the edge of the garden. At the front of the carriage were two magnificent horses, their glossy coats reflecting the moonlight.

One horse was a stunning dappled grey, its white coat speckled with a multitude of silver spots that shimmered in the gentle light. Its mane and tail were a soft, silken white, flowing beautifully as it shifted its weight and snorted softly, the sound almost musical.

The other horse was a deep, rich chestnut colour, its coat smooth and gleaming like polished bronze. Its mane and tail were darker, almost black, and it stood with a quiet dignity, its large, expressive eyes showing a gentle intelligence. Both horses had a calm, serene demeanour. They stood patiently, occasionally flicking their ears or softly nuzzling each other.

"This is Apollo," Mr Merrifield said, his voice filled with affection as he stroked the dappled horse's neck. "And this fine fellow is Artemis," he added, patting the chestnut horse's side. "They are as gentle as they are beautiful. I named them after the Greek gods of the sun and the moon, for their spirits seem to embody both light and darkness."

"Divine names for divine creatures," Claudia murmured in awe.

She reached out tentatively to stroke Apollo's velvety muzzle. When the horse nuzzled her hand gently, she grinned at the unexpected heat of his breath. Mr Merrifield watched her, clearly pleased by the connection she was making with his beloved horses.

"Indeed," he said. "These gentlemen are more than mere adornments to my carriage. They are cherished friends, and I care for them deeply. Last night, when I left the ball so suddenly, it was because my driver had urgently signalled to me. It turned out that Artemis had taken ill. He's much better now, but at the time, I had no choice but to attend to the matter immediately. I hope you can understand my predicament."

Moved by his obvious compassion, Claudia felt a swell of admiration for the man beside her.

"Your dedication to their welfare is most commendable, Mr Merrifield," she said earnestly. "In a world where so many view animals as mere possessions, your kindness is truly remarkable."

"Artemis and Apollo have been with me for many years now," Mr Merrifield said, his voice filled with affection. "They're not just carriage horses to me; they're my trusted companions."

Claudia found herself so drawn to Mr Merrifield as she listened to him speak passionately about his horses. His caring nature and deep sense of responsibility towards these animals seemed rare among the gentlemen she had encountered in society. The realisation stirred something within her – an attraction beyond mere physical appearance. She felt her cheeks reddening again, despite the coolness of the night air.

"Mr Merrifield," she said, a little shy, but keen to express her thoughts. "I must say that your devotion to your horses is both admirable and... endearing. It is a quality that I find most appealing."

"Miss Florence," said Mr Merrifield, a tender smile gracing his lips, "your kind words mean more to me than you may realise. To be appreciated for who I truly am – and not simply for my social standing or wealth – is a rare gift. I am honoured that you see this aspect of me."

Unsure of what to say, Claudia stood in silence, watching as Mr Merrifield moved to address his footman.

"Thank you once again for your excellent care of the horses, Robert," he said. "They are in the finest hands with you."

"It is my pleasure, Mr Merrifield," the footman replied. "They're fine animals, sir."

"Indeed they are," said Mr Merrifield. "Good evening to you, Robert. I trust you'll enjoy the rest of your night."

"Good evening, sir," Robert replied, seeming pleased to be acknowledged.

Claudia marvelled at the ease with which Mr Merrifield treated those in his employ. He seemed entirely devoid of the haughty arrogance she had so often seen among men of his status. It puzzled her that such a man existed. She found herself inexplicably drawn to him.

"Miss Florence," Mr Merrifield said, turning back towards her, "would you care to sit for a while? The stars are quite lovely tonight."

"Indeed, I would be delighted, Mr Merrifield," Claudia replied as she accepted his outstretched hand.

They walked together to a nearby bench, nestled amidst the fragrant blooms of the garden where they settled themselves beneath the celestial tapestry above.

As they sat, their conversation flowed effortlessly, touching upon subjects both light and profound. With each passing moment, Claudia felt an unfamiliar sense of joy blossoming within her chest, a sensation that both thrilled and frightened her. Was this the stirrings of affection that she had heard her sister Emily speak of?

"Mr Merrifield," she ventured hesitantly, "have you ever... felt a connection with someone that you did not expect?"

Mr Merrifield looked thoughtful for a moment before answering.

"Yes, Miss Florence. I have. Life has a way of surprising us, does it not? Sometimes, even when we least expect it, we find ourselves drawn to another soul – as if by an invisible thread."

Astounded by his words, Claudia sensed the presence of a kindred spark, a shared vulnerability that spoke to the understanding between them.

"Thank you for sharing that with me, Mr Merrifield," she said. "Your words give me hope that perhaps… perhaps there may be someone out there who can see past my insecurities and truly appreciate me for who I am."

"Miss Florence," Mr Merrifield said softly, his voice resonating with candour, "anyone would be a fool not to recognise your beauty – both inside and out. You are a remarkable woman, and I feel privileged to have spent this enchanted evening in your company."

As they continued to talk beneath the starlit sky, Claudia felt a burgeoning sense of wonder. For the first time in her life, she allowed herself to entertain the notion that perhaps in the eyes of one extraordinary man, she was truly seen.

Chapter Nine

The sun hung high in the cloudless sky, its golden rays filtering through the leaves of ancient oak trees and casting intricate patterns of light and shadow on the meticulously manicured lawns of the Duke of Pembroke's London estate. With a delicate glass of lemonade in her hand, Claudia wandered among the guests, her pale blue gown billowing softly. With each step, the memory of her time with Mr Merrifield at the previous two balls lingered in her mind.

The air was alive with the heady scent of blooming roses and the melodic symphony of cheerful chatter, creating an idyllic backdrop for the garden party. Claudia's mother stood at the edge of the gathering, resplendent in a gown of lime green, her smile radiant as she observed her daughter mingling with a little more confidence than she had before. Claudia returned the smile, grateful for her mother's silent encouragement amidst the sea of faces.

Yet, despite the beauty of the surroundings and pleasant summer breeze that teased her curls, a sense of unease began to creep over Claudia. She couldn't help but notice the subtle glances exchanged between some of the guests, the whispered conversations that ceased abruptly when she drew near. Was it her imagination, or did their smiles falter ever so slightly when they greeted her?

Approaching a cluster of ladies gathered beneath a blossoming cherry tree, Claudia's steps faltered as she inadvertently overheard snippets of conversation.

"...heard she was engaged once, you know..."

"...scandalous affair, I'm told..."

"...quite the mystery, that Miss Florence..."

Shocked, and certain that she had heard her name, Claudia yearned to confront the gossiping women, to demand an explanation for their hurtful words. She recoiled, however, at the thought of causing a scene. It wasn't in her nature to engage in confrontation, to draw attention to herself in such a public manner. The mere thought of calling them out on their gossip caused her cheeks to flush with embarrassment.

Besides, what good would it do? Confronting them would only draw further attention to the rumour – whatever it may be, fuelling its spread and adding credence to the malicious whispers that circulated among the guests.

Her heart plummeted like a stone as the pieces fell into place. Something unpleasant had evidently taken root, and was spreading like wildfire through the gossip-hungry circles of the London season. Overwhelmingly uncomfortable with the very fact that her name was on the lips of others, Claudia trembled, her breath catching in her throat as the discomfort of accusation settled over her like a heavy cloak.

Who could have done such a thing?! She had her suspicions, but couldn't be sure, and didn't want to wrongly accuse anyone. The thought of confronting a perpetrator filled her with equal parts indignation and fear.

What would Mr Merrifield think of her now? The memory of their shared dance, the thought of his hand on hers, his kindness, now felt like a distant dream, overshadowed by the dark cloud of suspicion that hung over her.

Lost in her turmoil, Claudia barely noticed as the lively chatter of the garden party faded into a distant hum. Tears pricked at her eyes, threatening to spill over as she struggled to maintain her composure amidst the flurry of activity surrounding her.

Try as she might, she knew she couldn't bear another moment in the suffocating atmosphere of the gathering. Despite her best efforts, with a deep sadness, she excused herself, offering polite smiles to those who glanced in her direction as she made her way towards one of the carriages waiting at the edge of the estate.

As she neared the carriage, Claudia spotted a footman standing nearby, his uniform impeccably pressed and his demeanour stoic. Swallowing back a sob, she approached him.

"Please... please inform Lady Beatrice Florence that her youngest daughter has left the garden party," she instructed, her words choked with emotion. "Tell her I shall be returning to our London residence."

The footman nodded silently, his expression unreadable as he turned to carry out her request. With a final glance over her shoulder, Claudia climbed into the waiting carriage.

Alone in the dimly lit interior, she allowed herself to succumb to an overwhelming tide of upset. She buried her face in her hands, finally allowing the tears to fall.

As the carriage lurched into motion, carrying her away from the garden party and the unpleasant atmosphere, Claudia's pained sobs echoed in the empty space, a poignant symphony of despair. Despite not knowing the precise details of the rumour that had tarnished her reputation, she couldn't deny its existence. The whispers, the sidelong glances, the hushed conversations: all were evidence enough of the vindictive gossip that could spread like wildfire through the ranks of London society.

As the rhythmic clatter of hooves against

cobblestones provided a backdrop to her turbulent thoughts, Claudia replayed the snippets of conversation she had overheard. Though fragmented and incomplete, the words carried enough weight to leave her in no doubt of their intent. Talk of an engagement, broken off under scandalous circumstances; a suggestion of impropriety, of whispered secrets and hidden truths: the whole thing had left her feeling dreadful, a cold knot of discomfort tightening in her throat.

Though she couldn't be certain of the specifics, Claudia knew that the damage had been done. The mere suggestion of scandal was enough to tarnish her reputation, casting doubt on her character and integrity before the entire ton. And while part of her longed to refute the rumours, to set the record straight and clear her name of any wrongdoing, she knew that such efforts could be futile, for in the court of public opinion, perception often outweighed truth, and once the seeds of doubt had been sown, they would always be difficult to uproot.

Claudia could only steel herself against the storm of speculation and innuendo, clinging to the hope that those who knew her best would see through the lies and stand by her in her hour of need.

Chapter Ten

As soon as the carriage came to a halt outside the Florence family's London residence, Claudia hastily descended the steps, her skirts rustling with each urgent stride. She barely acknowledged the footman who had opened the door for her, her mind solely focused on reaching the sanctuary of her chamber. As she ascended the grand staircase of the large house, it seemed endless, her breath coming in shallow gasps, her mind whirling from the discomfort and turbulence of the garden party.

Reaching her chamber, she pushed open the door and quickly closed it behind her, the solid click of the latch providing a small sense of relief. She leaned against the door for a moment in an effort to regain her composure. The quiet of the room enveloped her, a stark contrast to the murmurs and whispers that had plagued her earlier.

With a sigh, she moved to the window, the sunlight filtering in through the net curtains. She sank onto the window seat. A cushioned alcove, it offered a comforting refuge where she could gather her thoughts.

She gazed out at the bustling streets below, where the gentle hum of London life continued unabated, oblivious to her turmoil. Equally, her mind was far from the lively scene outside. How dare someone spread such a horrible rumour?

Having cried so hard in the carriage, Claudia was out of tears. The emotional exhaustion that had weighed her down began to give way to a simmering anger, indignation rising within her, overwhelming the sadness and replacing it with a fierce fury.

She stood abruptly, catching sight of her reflection in the vanity mirror. Studying her tear-streaked face and dishevelled hair, she could still hear the echo of whispered conversations as she recalled the subtle glances cast in her direction. It wasn't enough that she had to navigate the pressures of the season; now, she had to contend with this vile slander as well.

As her thoughts swirled, Claudia was abruptly taken aback by a stern knock at her chamber door. The sound was sharp, cutting through her reverie and causing her to wince.

"Claudia?" came her mother's voice, the tone a mixture of annoyance and concern.

Claudia hesitated for a moment before responding.

"Yes, Mother?"

The door opened, and Beatrice stepped into the room, her eyes searching Claudia's for answers.

"Why did you leave the garden party so abruptly?" Beatrice demanded as she closed the door behind her. "Do you have any idea how improper it is to leave without informing anyone? You know how important these events are."

Claudia looked down, her fingers twisting in the fabric of her skirts.

"I'm sorry, Mother. I... I wasn't feeling well."

"You seemed fine before you left," said Beatrice, clearly unsatisfied with the vague response. "What happened? Why are you so upset?"

Claudia bit her lip, unsure of how much to reveal. She then took a deep breath, trying to steady her voice.

"It's nothing, really. Just... something someone said. It bothered me more than it should have."

Beatrice's expression softened, her irritation giving way to unease. She stepped closer, reaching out to gently lift Claudia's chin.

"Tell me, Claudia. What was said?"

Claudia's eyes welled up again, but she blinked back the tears. She didn't want to cry in front of her mother.

"There are rumours, Mother: untrue and hurtful things have been said about me. I didn't want to cause a scene, so I left."

Beatrice's expression darkened with a mixture of anger and protectiveness.

"Who started these rumours? What are they saying?"

"I don't know who started them," Claudia answered, her voice laced with shame, "but they claim I was engaged before, and that it ended in scandal. It's all lies."

Beatrice's grip on Claudia's chin tightened slightly, and then she released her, her demeanour hardening with resolve.

"We will get to the bottom of this, Claudia. No one will spread falsehoods about you without consequences. You must not let them see that their lies have hurt you. We must show them that we Florences are stronger than their petty gossip."

A sudden knock on Claudia's chamber door interrupted the tension in the room. Claudia and Beatrice exchanged a glance.

"Who could that be?" Beatrice murmured, her voice tinged with impatience.

Before Claudia could respond, the door opened, and Emily stepped inside, her face set in a determined expression.

"Emily?" Claudia said, her surprise evident. "What are you doing here?"

Emily closed the door behind her and crossed the room with purposeful strides.

"I know what the rumour is," she announced firmly, getting straight to the point. "And I know who started it."

"You must tell us," Beatrice demanded, a flicker of discomfort passing over her features.

"Miss Jacqueline Harcourt," said Emily, her tone edged with anger. "She's the one spreading lies about Claudia."

"What has she said?" Beatrice asked.

Claudia's breath caught as Emily cast her an apologetic glance.

"Miss Harcourt is telling everyone that Claudia was previously engaged, and that the engagement was broken off under scandalous circumstances. She's implying that there's something disreputable in Claudia's past."

"What exactly is she saying?" Beatrice pressed.

"Miss Harcourt, with her cunning and talent for weaving believable tales, claims that Claudia was engaged to Mr Henry Ashcroft," Emily elaborated, anger still brimming in her words. "She says that Mr Ashcroft discovered certain… unsavoury details about Claudia's character, and broke off the engagement in a fit of moral outrage."

"That's completely untrue!" Claudia snapped, furious at the audacity. "I've never even met Mr Ashcroft!"

"I know, Claudia," said Emily, "but Miss Harcourt's story is gaining traction. She's even embellishing it further, saying that Mr Ashcroft caught you in a compromising situation, though she doesn't specify what it was. She's also spreading whispers about intimate letters exchanged between you two, suggesting that Mr Ashcroft had no choice but to end the betrothal."

Claudia felt her knees weaken, and she sank back onto the window seat. The room seemed to close in around her, the air thick with the weight of Emily's words. Beatrice, her face pale with apprehension, reached out to steady herself against the back of a chair.

"Why would Miss Harcourt do such a thing?" Beatrice demanded, her voice trembling with a blend of rage and distress. "Claudia has done nothing to deserve this."

"She's jealous, Mother," said Emily. "Jealous that Claudia has caught the attention of the dashing Mr Luke Merrifield. Miss Harcourt seems determined to ruin Claudia's chances out of spite."

Claudia buried her face in her hands, the enormity of the situation crashing over her.

"What am I going to do?" she pleaded, her voice choked with emotion. "How can I face anyone now?"

"We'll think of something," Emily said softly, moving to Claudia's side and placing a reassuring hand on her shoulder. "We cannot allow Miss Harcourt to get away with this."

"That's right," said Beatrice, regaining some of her composure. "We must find a way to set the record straight. Claudia, you have nothing to be ashamed of. We'll make sure everyone knows the truth."

Chapter Eleven

Claudia's slender fingers traced the intricate embroidery of her bedspread as she sat alone in her chamber. The weak morning light filtered in through the curtains, casting a muted glow upon the room and accentuating the shadows of her delicate features. Her eyes, usually so expressive and bright, were dull with fatigue from a restless night spent tossing and turning, her mind racing with the cruel rumour that Miss Harcourt had so maliciously spread.

"Miss Florence," a soft voice announced.

Claudia turned to see Jemima, who was standing patiently in the doorway, a look of concern on her face.

"I have come to help you dress."

"Thank you, Jemima. Do come in," said Claudia, hesitant for the day ahead, but still grateful to see her kind maid. "I fear I did not sleep well last night."

"Your sister has informed me of the situation," Jemima said with sympathy as she entered the room. "I sense she has been quite disturbed by the nature of the rumour. She seems determined to put an end to Miss Harcourt's gossip and defend your honour."

"Truly?" Claudia asked, her voice wavering with a mixture of hope and disbelief. "I had wondered if her intentions were more about preserving the family name than protecting me. Perhaps I have underestimated her."

"I am inclined to believe that your sister cares for you deeply," Jemima assured, placing a comforting hand on Claudia's shoulder. "She may not always show it, but maybe that's just her way. She is, after all, a very sociable woman with many things to attend to."

Claudia appreciated Jemima's candour. In moments of such turmoil, it often came as a relief, offering a refreshing and valuable perspective.

As she rose slowly from her sitting position on the bed, her movements languid and heavy, the delicate lace of Claudia's nightgown brushed against her ankles, a soft whisper in the quiet room. Walking over to the vanity, she caught sight of her reflection in the mirror. She looked exhausted.

"Don't worry, Miss," Jemima said, as though she had read Claudia's mind. "I'm here to help."

Claudia took a seat in a simple chair by the vanity, its wooden frame polished to a soft gloss. The cushion was firm yet comfortable. She settled herself, smoothing the lower half of her nightgown before folding her hands in her lap.

Jemima moved behind her, picking up a silver-handled brush from the vanity. Familiar and at ease with the process, she began to work it through Claudia's hair, the bristles gliding smoothly through the tangled strands. The rhythmic motion was soothing, a gentle, repetitive cadence that helped to quieten Claudia's mind.

As Jemima brushed, Claudia could feel the

tension in her scalp slowly beginning to ease. It was the first time her hair had been brushed since she had got out of bed; the sensation was both comforting and grounding. Jemima's touch was deft and gentle, careful not to tug or pull too harshly.

Claudia's mind wandered back to the dreadful rumour that had been spread about her. She couldn't bear the thought of facing anyone this social season, knowing that the gossip would follow her everywhere she went. The very idea of stepping into another ballroom or attending another garden party filled her with a sense of dread that tightened around her chest like a vice.

More than the social fallout, however, what pained Claudia the most was the thought of Mr Merrifield. She cherished the time they had spent together at the two balls, those precious moments filled with growing affection. The memory of their dance still lingered in her mind, the way his touch had been so gentle, and his smile so reassuring. She remembered the way they had sat under the stars, speaking of dreams and futures, and of how he had introduced her to his beloved horses, Apollo and Artemis.

But now, all of that seemed like a distant dream, overshadowed by the scandalous lies that had been spread about her. Claudia's heart ached at the possibility that Mr Merrifield might believe the rumours, that he might see her as someone unworthy of his affection. She had been so sure that they were developing feelings for each other, and the thought of losing that burgeoning connection was almost too much. As Jemima's brush moved through her hair with gentle precision, Claudia had to force herself to keep still, her hands clasped tightly in her lap.

"Miss Florence," Jemima began hesitantly, sensing Claudia's need for distraction, "would you like to share your thoughts? It may help to ease the burden."

"Jemima," Claudia said, her brow furrowing, "do you truly believe that such rumours will dissipate?"

"Miss, I have every faith that the truth shall prevail," Jemima said. "You are innocent, and soon enough, the gossip will lose its appeal."

"I do hope you're right," Claudia said sadly.

Although she attempted to draw strength from Jemima's unwavering belief in her, Claudia couldn't help but wonder whether Mr Merrifield would still desire her company after hearing such scandalous tales. The delicate warmth she'd felt in his presence now seemed tainted by Miss Harcourt's spite.

Chapter Twelve

Grateful that the day ahead would demand no presence at any social events, Claudia had remained in her chamber all morning. After Jemima had left, she had settled back into her solitude. As the sun had climbed higher in the sky, casting rays of lemon through the lace curtains, she had hardly noticed.

Sitting by the window, she stared out at the bustling street below, the distant sounds of carriages and pedestrians reaching her ears. It was a small comfort to know that, at least for today, she didn't have to face prying eyes and whispered conversations from the ton.

Each tick of the clock served to remind Claudia of the uncertainty that now clouded her future. Her thoughts kept returning to Mr Merrifield, to the two magical evenings they had shared at the balls. The memory of his smile and kind eyes was both a balm and a torment. She couldn't help but wonder if he had heard the rumours, and if he believed them. The thought that he might turn away from her, repelled by the lies, was devastating.

She leaned back in her seat, closing her eyes for a moment, seeking some semblance of calm. The events of the past few days played over and over in her mind, each recollection sharpening her pain.

At least in the safety of her chamber, she thought, she could almost pretend that everything was normal.

"Claudia?"

It was the voice of her mother, accompanied by a sudden knock at the chamber door. Both broke the silence that hung heavy in the air.

"What is it, Mother?"

"May I speak with you?"

"Yes, of course," Claudia conceded. "Come in."

Beatrice opened the door. As she stood at the threshold of the chamber, her expression softened ever so slightly when her eyes met Claudia's.

"Mr Merrifield is here," she said, her tone measured and careful. "He has come to the house, requesting to speak with you."

Claudia blinked in surprise. She couldn't fathom why Mr Merrifield would want to see her now, after everything that had transpired. Surely he must have heard the rumours spread by Miss Harcourt. She assumed that, on such basis, he would want to make it clear that he no longer wished to have anything to do with her. She was too afraid to hope otherwise.

"Mother..." Claudia said nervously, wringing her hands together. "Do you truly believe it's wise for me to see him – after all that has been said and done?"

Beatrice studied Claudia for a moment, taking in the uncertainty etched upon her face. Though stern in demeanour, she was not without compassion; the sight of her daughter's anguish moved her deeply.

"Sometimes, my child," she said gently, "the only way to dispel a falsehood is to confront it. If Mr Merrifield has come to you in search of the truth, then it is your duty – and your right – to set the record straight. Do not allow Miss Harcourt's deceit to destroy what might have been."

With a shuddering breath, Claudia nodded in agreement, her resolve strengthened by her mother's words. She would meet with Mr Merrifield, if only to find out the consequences that awaited her. No matter how difficult the conversation may turn out to be, she owed it to herself – and to him – to show her face.

"Very well," she murmured, rising from her seat. "I shall speak with Mr Merrifield."

"Bravely spoken, my dear," Beatrice said, her eyes glimmering with pride as they locked onto Claudia's. "And remember, I shall be close, should you need me."

"Thank you, Mother," Claudia said humbly.

As they descended the stairs, Claudia's heart thundered in her chest like a wild stallion, threatening to escape its confines. She could scarcely believe that Mr Merrifield was truly downstairs, seeking her company despite the awful rumours that had been circulating. A wave of panic washed over her as she imagined his handsome face clouded with disappointment and disdain.

"Mother, I cannot," Claudia whispered, her voice trembling with fear. "Surely he has come to sever all ties with me – to tell me to stay away from him forevermore."

"Dearest, you mustn't think so negatively," Beatrice admonished. "You have no way of knowing Mr Merrifield's intentions until you speak with him."

Taking a steadying breath, Claudia squared her shoulders, desperately trying to keep her emotions under control. She did her best to continue stoically with her mother down the grand staircase, each step bringing them closer to the drawing room where Mr Merrifield was waiting.

As they approached the door, Claudia could feel the heavy weight of doubt settling upon her. Her thoughts raced with fears and uncertainties, painting a bleak picture of the impending encounter in her mind's eye. Surely Mr Merrifield would cast her aside now, convinced that her tarnished reputation would mar his own spotless image.

"Remember, my dear, to present yourself with grace and courage," Beatrice murmured convincingly. "No matter what transpires, you are still a lady of refinement and dignity."

"Thank you, Mother," Claudia replied softly, grateful for her mother's unwavering support.

As the two women entered the drawing room together, the sight of Mr Merrifield took Claudia's breath away. Seated in an elegantly upholstered chair near the window, his eyes, a deep shade of blue that seemed to hold the secrets of the ocean itself, met hers with an intensity that sent shivers down her spine. Despite the turmoil of emotions swirling within her, she couldn't help but feel the magnetic pull of attraction.

"Miss Florence," he said, rising from his seat with a fluidity that bespoke concern for her feelings.

As he approached, the solemn energy emanating from him made it clear that his intentions were rooted solely in his care for Claudia, even if he was about to tell her something that she didn't want to hear.

"Mr Merrifield," Claudia replied, her voice wavering anxiously. "I... I... I don't know what to say."

"Please, Miss Florence," Mr Merrifield implored, the fervour in his voice catching Claudia off guard, "grant me a moment of your time. I am desperate to speak with you."

Claudia hesitated. She glanced at her mother for guidance. Beatrice nodded approvingly.

"Very well, Mr Merrifield," Beatrice said firmly. "I shall be in the adjoining room if you require anything further."

With that, Claudia's mother swept from the drawing room, closing the door behind her.

As Claudia stood alone with Mr Merrifield, the tension in the air seemed to thicken, the silence heavy. Taking a seat to try and steady herself, she clasped her hands tightly in her lap, her knuckles white with the force of her grip.

She looked up at Mr Merrifield, his gaze steady and unwavering. She swallowed hard.

"Mr Merrifield, I am desperately sad and sorry that you will no longer want to be involved with me," she said, her words tarred with regret.

"Miss Florence," he said, his voice gentle but full of conviction, "I cannot begin to express how deeply it pains me to hear that you are so troubled by these malicious rumours. I assure you, they hold no weight with me."

Surprised by his words, Claudia found herself struggling to contain the flood of emotions that threatened to overwhelm her. As she looked up at him, her eyes searching his for any sign of flippancy, all she found was sincerity and concern etched across his handsome features.

"Y-you mean you don't believe it?" she stammered.

"Of course not," he replied passionately. "I

have come here today to assure you of my unconditional trust and support. It is unthinkable that someone as kind and honest as yourself could be the subject of such slander."

Claudia felt her spirits soar, a renewed sense of hope blossoming within her. The thought that Mr Merrifield could see beyond the hurtful gossip and recognise her true nature filled her with a joyous sense of relief.

"Allow me to explain," Mr Merrifield implored, his voice steady despite the gravity of the situation. "I am well acquainted with Mr Henry Ashcroft. He has been travelling for the past eighteen months and is currently in Italy for the summer, which makes it impossible for him to have been involved in any scandal with you. Even if he were in England, I would not believe such a rumour. I know Mr Ashcroft well enough to be certain that what Miss Harcourt claims simply did not happen."

Claudia's heart swelled with relief, her eyes welling up. However, she then hesitated for a moment, her insecurities creeping back, igniting tendrils of doubt.

"But what if you did not know Mr Ashcroft?" she asked, not wishing to appear rude or defensive, but desperate for clarity. "What if he were here in England? Would you still believe in me? Or would you have been swayed by those spiteful whispers?"

The air between them seemed to crackle with friction. Claudia watched as Mr Merrifield's expression shifted. His eyes shimmered with emotion, a depth of feeling that both thrilled and terrified her.

He crouched down to look directly at her. She could scarcely believe this was happening. His hands, warm and gentle, reached out to cradle her face, his tender touch sending a wave of heat flooding through her. She felt her cheeks flush, her pulse quickening in a flurry of hope and fear.

"Miss Florence," he said, his voice low and filled with something she dared not name.

The way he said her name, so soft and reverent, made her feel deliciously weak. The heat of his palms against her skin was both grounding and electrifying. The world around them seemed to fade away, leaving only the two of them, locked in a fragile, tenuous connection. She ached with the intensity of her emotions, the longing to believe in the possibility of a future with him battling against her fear of rejection.

"I must assure you that I have never for a moment doubted my feelings for you," Mr Merrifield said firmly, his gaze seeming to pierce straight into Claudia's soul. "They are as constant and true as the North Star, unswayed by the idle gossip and malicious falsehoods that may swirl around us."

"Thank you, Mr Merrifield," Claudia whispered. "To know that you believe in me, despite everything... it means more than words can express."

"I'm glad," he said. "I want you to know that no matter what anyone else says, my feelings for you remain unchanged. The time we've spent together has shown me your true character, and I would be honoured to be by your side. Now that we have moved past these dreadful rumours, I would be delighted to escort you to Lord Worthington's garden party. It would be my greatest pleasure to spend more time with you, enjoying the festivities together."

Claudia felt the weight of the past few days beginning to lift. The malicious whispers that had haunted her seemed to fade into the background, overshadowed by Mr Merrifield's reassuring words. His offer to escort her to Lord Worthington's garden party wasn't just a simple gesture; it was a public declaration of his support and admiration, a statement to society that he was willing to stand by her.

"Mr Merrifield, I... I don't know what to say. Thank you. Truly, thank you."

"Miss Florence," he said. "I cannot help but feel that every moment spent with you is a gift I cherish. When I am near you, the world seems brighter, every shadow dispelled by the light of your presence. From the first dance we shared, I knew there was something extraordinary about you. Your kindness, the way you see the world... It has captivated me in ways I never thought possible."

Claudia couldn't help but hang on his every word. The depth of his feelings mirrored hers. He passionately clasped his hands around hers, his thumb brushing over her knuckles in a reassuring gesture.

"Claudia," he said, the formality dropping away in his earnest plea, "I long to spend more time with you, to be by your side through every ball, every garden party, every stolen moment beneath the stars. I yearn for the chance to show you just how much you mean to me, to prove that my intentions are true and that my affection is unwavering. Please, Claudia, cast your doubts aside. Please grant me this."

The smile in Claudia's eyes told him everything he needed to know. Her answer was a resounding yes.

Chapter Thirteen

The heavy oak doors of the Florence family's London residence closed with a soft thud, echoing through the foyer as Mr Merrifield departed. In the drawing room, Claudia stood in front of a tall window, her delicate fingers resting against the cool glass pane as she allowed her mind to wander, keen to process the strength of the conversation that had just taken place.

"I must say," Beatrice said as she entered the drawing room, distracting Claudia from her reverie, "I did not expect to see Mr Merrifield here today. Pray tell, what was the nature of his visit?"

Claudia suspected that her mother may have overheard more than a few snippets of the conversation between herself and Mr Merrifield. Nevertheless, considering that the conversation had been everything she had wanted it to be and more, she felt no hesitancy at the prospect of relaying it to her mother.

"Mother," she began, turning to face Beatrice. "Mr Merrifield came to speak with me about the rumours. He assured me that he knows them to be completely unfounded and that he does not believe them for a moment. In fact, he seemed most upset that such malice has been cast in my direction."

"Indeed," said Beatrice, a glimmer of pride flickering in her gaze. "And what else transpired between you two?"

"Mr Merrifield has confessed feelings for me, Mother," Claudia said, steadying herself before she continued. "He spoke of how deeply he cares for me, and of how he wishes to escort me to the upcoming garden party hosted by Lord Worthington."

"Ah," Beatrice said, assessing Claudia carefully. "You must have captured his heart then, my dear. This could be most advantageous for our family."

"Mother," Claudia objected, biting her lip as

she summoned the courage to voice her innermost thoughts. "I do not wish for this to be a matter of advantage or societal gain. My heart has been moved by Mr Merrifield's affection. I want to be with him for the love we share, not the status it may bring."

"Love," Beatrice said with a nostalgic sigh. "A rare and precious thing indeed. You are fortunate to have found it, Claudia."

"Thank you, Mother," Claudia said, touched by the tenderness in her mother's voice. "I only hope that our union will bring happiness to us both, and that society will accept us for who we truly are."

"I shall support you, my dear. Mr Merrifield is a fine gentleman. I must say that I approve of him," Beatrice assured. "He possesses qualities that are rare among the gentlemen of our society. He is kind-hearted, steadfast, and unafraid to defend your honour. It is clear to me that he cares for you deeply."

Claudia felt a rush of relief and gratitude. Amidst the joy and excitement of knowing that Mr Merrifield had affectionate feelings and wanted to spend more time with her, her mother's approval meant the world.

Chapter Fourteen

As the day of Lord Worthington's garden party approached, Claudia found herself bubbling with excitement. She imagined walking through the lush manicured grounds on Mr Merrifield's arm, sharing whispered conversations amidst the fragrant blooms. The thought of spending more time with him, of exploring this newfound connection, filled her with a happiness so vast that it was almost overwhelming.

In quieter moments, she allowed herself to relive the memory of Mr Merrifield's confession. His words of admiration, his yearning to be near her; they played over and over in her mind, each repetition bringing a fresh wave of pleasure. She felt a sense of validation, a deep affirmation that she was indeed worthy of love and respect.

With each passing day, her anticipation grew. She carefully selected her gown for the garden party, envisioning how she would feel to be by Mr Merrifield's side. The mere thought of his presence filled her with elation.

On the morning of the much anticipated day, the sun bathed the opulent drawing room in its golden embrace, casting a serene glow upon the delicate floral arrangements that adorned the space. Dressed impeccably in a gown of the softest periwinkle silk, Claudia stood by the tall window, her reflection mirrored in the polished glass.

"Miss Florence, you look absolutely radiant," Jemima said as she adjusted Claudia's hair one final time, securing an intricate ivory comb amidst her chestnut locks.

"Thank you, Jemima," Claudia said happily, now more willing to believe such complements than she had been at the beginning of the season.

"Miss Florence, Mr Merrifield has arrived," announced a footman from the doorway, his voice crisp and formal.

"Thank you, James," Claudia responded, practically leaping at the news.

She smoothed her gown, the exquisite fabric rustling softly beneath her fingers as she made her way to the front door.

Once outside, as she descended the steps, Claudia caught sight of Mr Merrifield. Standing patiently outside his carriage, he was clad in a finely tailored coat and breeches, his dark hair framing his handsome face. When their eyes locked, he offered Claudia a reassuring smile.

"Miss Florence, you are a vision of loveliness," he said, his voice smooth and sincere as he took her hand to assist her down the final steps.

"Thank you, Mr Merrifield," she replied, aware of the emerging heat in her cheeks. "I am delighted that you are taking me to the garden party."

"Nothing would give me greater pleasure," he said.

"I see you've brought your horses."

"Indeed," he said proudly. "They do enjoy their work, and I know they'll be pleased to see you again."

Claudia walked to greet the horses. Apollo nickered softly, his grey and white flecked ears pricking forward in recognition. Artemis, his chestnut coat shining in the sun, snorted gently, his large, expressive eyes watching Claudia.

Claudia reached out, her fingers brushing over Apollo's soft muzzle. The horse leaned into her touch, a contented rumble emanating from his chest. She then moved to Artemis, who nudged her hand with his velvet nose, as if asking for the same gentle attention.

"It's good to see you too, Apollo, Artemis," Claudia said as she ran her hand down Artemis' neck.

Mr Merrifield watched their interaction, a grin spreading across his face.

"They seem to have taken quite a liking to you, Miss Florence," he said happily. "They're good judges of character. They know kindness when they see it."

Claudia graciously accepted as Mr Merrifield escorted her into the carriage. Once inside, she marvelled at the luxurious velvet upholstery. As they settled into their seats, she could not help but feel a sense of awe.

As the carriage began to move, its gentle sway rocked them into a companionable silence. Claudia allowed herself to be lulled by the rhythmic motion, her thoughts drifting to the garden party that awaited them and the precious moments they would share in each other's company. In some ways, however, the world outside their cocoon seemed distant and unimportant.

"Are you looking forward to Lord Worthington's garden party?" Mr Merrifield asked, his voice soothing to Claudia.

"Indeed, I am," she replied. "Your presence makes the prospect infinitely more wonderful."

As her eyes met his for a fleeting glance, Claudia felt the beginnings of another blush in her cheeks. In a moment of shyness, she quickly looked away. She had never felt this way about anyone before.

Seemingly endeared by this, a smile played at the corners of Mr Merrifield's mouth.

"Your company is equally delightful, Miss Florence," he assured her. "We shall face this day together and not let anyone or anything tarnish our enjoyment."

Chapter Fifteen

The exuberant laughter and lilting music intermingled with the delicate fragrance of roses that enveloped the garden. Stepping out of the carriage with Mr Merrifield, Claudia felt her spirits soar in anticipation of the delights that awaited them.

"Miss Florence," Mr Merrifield said, his mannerisms charming as he offered her his arm, "may I have the honour of escorting you to this splendid scene?"

"Indeed, Mr Merrifield," Claudia replied excitedly.

As they began to make their way towards the heart of the festivities, a hush fell over the crowd, causing Claudia to feel anxious.

"Pay them no attention," Mr Merrifield murmured assertively in her ear. "I'm proud to be here with you."

Despite Claudia's presence, several young ladies cast longing glances at Mr Merrifield, their fan-fluttering and coquettish expressions betraying their interest. Amongst them, Miss Harcourt stood out like a viper amidst butterflies, her eyes narrowing as they darted between the pair.

Refusing to acknowledge the adoring stares targeted in his direction, Mr Merrifield's attention remained steadfastly on Claudia. Wasting no time, he strode purposefully through the throng of admirers, his arm never straying from hers. The whispers that followed in his wake were like a summer breeze, barely registering with him.

Despite Mr Merrifield's intentions and Claudia's best wishes, however, as they headed towards a beautifully arranged table display of sumptuous-looking cakes, Miss Harcourt and her gaggle of friends began to approach with predatory grins.

"Fear not, Miss Florence," Mr Merrifield

whispered to her. "I shall not allow any harm to come to your reputation or your spirits."

"Why, Mr Merrifield," said Miss Harcourt, her tone saccharine, her insincerity dripping from every syllable, "it is such a pleasure to see you again. And Miss Florence, you look... well."

"Miss Harcourt," Mr Merrifield acknowledged curtly, bracing himself for the inevitable barbs.

"Tell me, Mr Merrifield," Miss Harcourt continued, feigning nonchalance, "have you not asked Miss Florence many questions? I'm sure she has an interesting story or two to tell about her past, for I hear it has been most eventful."

Claudia felt her cheeks flame at Miss Harcourt's sheer audacity, but she held her ground. Glancing at Mr Merrifield, she silently pleaded for him to put an end to her torment.

"Miss Harcourt," Mr Merrifield said sharply, unrelenting in his desire to get straight to the point, "I am well aware of the falsehoods that you may wish to tell me about Miss Florence. I am confident that they hold no water."

Miss Harcourt faltered for a moment before attempting to regain her composure, but Mr Merrifield pressed on, his voice steely.

"Miss Florence is a lady of impeccable character, and I will not tolerate any attempts to besmirch her reputation."

"Very well, Mr Merrifield," Miss Harcourt muttered, her cheeks flushed with embarrassment. "I shall refrain from discussing the matter further."

"See that you do," Mr Merrifield warned, his hold firm on Claudia's arm.

Miss Harcourt nodded, her cheeks still crimson. She hastily retreated with her entourage in tow, leaving Claudia standing tall amidst the whispers and side glances of the surrounding guests.

With the confrontation behind them, Mr Merrifield happily escorted Claudia around, her mood lighter and her spirits lifted. In full swing, Lord Worthington's garden party was a kaleidoscope of colour and fun. The many guests, in all their afternoon finery, gathered under the gazebos, conversing companionably.

Mr Merrifield then guided Claudia to a quieter corner of the garden where a picturesque fountain gurgled serenely, its cool waters sparkling in the sunlight.

"Shall we explore?" he suggested playfully.

Claudia nodded eagerly.

"I'd like that very much," she said.

They wandered along the garden paths, pausing to admire the intricate floral arrangements and marvel at the artistry of the topiaries. Mr Merrifield pointed out various plants and flowers, sharing snippets of botanical knowledge that fascinated Claudia and drew her deeper into the moment. His enthusiasm was infectious. She found herself laughing more freely than she had in a long time.

They stopped at a gazebo draped in ivy, where a string quartet played a gentle melody. Mr Merrifield procured a plate of delicate pastries and fruits, and they sat together, delighting in the sweet treats and the music. Claudia savoured the simple pleasure of his company, feeling an ever-deepening connection.

"I've never enjoyed a garden party quite this much," she confessed. "It feels... magical."

Mr Merrifield reached out, taking her hand in his.

"I feel the same way," he said. "Being here with you makes everything feel more vivid, more alive."

As the afternoon progressed, they joined in with a spirited game of croquet, their playful banter and easy rapport drawing smiles from those around them. Claudia's laughter rang out, clear and joyful, as Mr Merrifield guided her through the game, his touch gentle and reassuring.

Later, they strolled by the ornamental lake, watching swans glide seamlessly across the water. As the sun began its slow descent, casting a golden hue over the garden and enveloping them in its embrace, they sat down together on a secluded bench beneath a grand oak tree.

"Thank you for standing by me today," Claudia said softly, her eyes meeting his.

"The pleasure is all mine, Miss Florence. I must admit that our time together has been nothing short of enchanting. Your grace and wit have captivated me completely. I find myself yearning for your company more each day."

A pause hung in the air. The world seemed to hold its breath, the moment suspended in a delicate balance. Mr Merrifield looked at Claudia with an intensity that astounded her.

"Claudia," he began, his voice impassioned as he took her hands in his. "I've been searching for the right words, the right moment to tell you what's been in my heart since the first night we met... I didn't used to believe in love at first sight, but now I do. Every moment we've spent together, every shared glance and whispered word, has only deepened my feelings for you. I can do nothing but yearn for you."

Claudia gazed in awe at the incredible man beside her. He leaned in closer, his eyes never leaving hers.

"Claudia," he implored, "I want nothing more than to spend the rest of my life with you, to wake up each morning knowing that you are mine and I am yours. I've dreamed of this moment, imagined it a thousand times, but nothing compares to the reality of having you here with me now."

He took a deep breath, preparing himself for what he wanted to say next.

"I know it's soon, and I know the weight of what I'm asking, but my heart cannot wait any longer. Claudia Florence, will you do me the honour of becoming my wife? Will you marry me and make me the happiest man in the world?"

Claudia's chest tightened with an overwhelming feeling of euphoria. The sincerity and depth of the proposal had left her speechless. She could see the genuine desire in this wonderful man's eyes, the vulnerability and hope that mirrored her own.

"Yes," she said, her voice a breath of pure emotion. "Yes, Luke Merrifield, I want to marry you – more than anything."

His face broke into the most radiant smile. He then pulled Claudia into a soulful embrace. As they held each other, it felt as though everything in the world was just right.

In that moment, beneath the ancient oak tree, surrounded by the beauty of the garden and the warmth of their shared love, Claudia knew that this was just the beginning of a lifetime of happiness and passion with the man who had captured her heart so completely.

www.ingramcontent.com/pod-product-compliance
Lightning Source LLC
Chambersburg PA
CBHW061454210726

48287CB00007B/2499